THE SCARECROW'S HAT

For Ruth

Copyright ©2000 by Ken Brown.
This paperback edition first published in 2002 by Andersen Press Ltd.
The rights of Ken Brown to be identified as the author and illustrator of this work
have been asserted by him in accordance with the Copyright, Designs and Patents Act, 1988.
First published in Great Britain in 2000 by Andersen Press Ltd. 20 Vauxhall Bridge Road, London SW1V 2SA.
Published in Australia by Random House Australia Pty., 20 Alfred Street, Milsons Point, Sydney, NSW 2061.
All rights reserved. Colour separated in Switzerland by Photolitho AG, Zurich.
Printed and bound in Italy by Grafiche AZ, Verona.

10 9 8 7 6 5 4 3 2

British Library Cataloguing in Publication Data available.

ISBN 1 84270 101 0

This book has been printed on acid-free paper

THE SCARECROW'S HAT

Written and illustrated by
Ken Brown

Andersen Press
London

"That's a nice hat," said Chicken to the scarecrow.

"Yes, it is," replied the scarecrow, "but I'd rather have a walking stick. I've been standing here for years and my arms are so tired. I'd love a walking stick to lean on. I'd swap my hat for a walking stick any day."

Now Chicken didn't have a walking stick, but she knew someone who did.

"That's a nice walking stick," said Chicken to the badger.

"Yes, it is," replied the badger, "but I'd rather have a piece of ribbon. It gets hot and stuffy underground so I prop my door open with my stick, but I'm always tripping over it. If I had a ribbon I could *tie* the door open. I'd swap my walking stick for a ribbon any day."

Now Chicken didn't have a ribbon, but she knew someone who did.

"That's a nice ribbon," said Chicken to the jackdaw.

"Yes, it is," said the jackdaw," but I'd rather have some wool. My nest is on this high, stone ledge and it's very hard to sit on. I'd love some warm, soft wool to line it with. I'd swap this ribbon for some wool any day."

Now Chicken didn't have any wool, but she knew someone who did.

"That's a nice wool coat," said Chicken to the sheep.

"Yes, it is," replied the sheep, "but I'd rather have a pair of glasses.
I have to keep a look out for the wolf and my eyes are not as good as they
used to be. I really need a pair of glasses. I'd swap some of my wool for
a pair of glasses any day."

Now Chicken didn't have a pair of glasses,
but she knew someone who did.

"That's a nice pair of glasses," said Chicken to the owl.

"Yes, it is," replied the owl. "My old ones broke, so I had to get a new pair. But I'd rather have a blanket. The sun streams through my window and keeps me awake all day, which wouldn't matter if I had a good thick blanket to sleep under. I'd swap my glasses for a blanket any day."

Now Chicken didn't have a blanket, but she knew someone who did.

"That's a nice blanket," said Chicken to the donkey.

"Yes, it is," replied the donkey. "But I'd rather have a few feathers. The flies drive me mad, buzzing round my ears. My tail isn't quite long enough to flick them away, but if I had some long feathers tied to the end of it, I could swat them easily. I'd swap my blanket for a few long feathers any day.

Quick as a flash, Chicken pulled out one, two, three of her longest feathers and tied them to the donkey's tail.

The donkey was delighted and, true to his word, swapped his blanket
for the feathers.

Chicken took the blanket to the owl —
who swapped it for his glasses (the old ones, of course).

She took the glasses to the sheep —
who swapped them for her wool.

She took the wool to the jackdaw —
who swapped it for her ribbon.

She took the ribbon to the badger —
who swapped it for his walking stick.

Finally, she took the walking stick to the scarecrow.
With a grateful sigh of relief, he leant his tired old arms on the stick
and gladly swapped it for his battered old hat.

Chicken took the hat and filled it with fresh, sweet-smelling straw. . .

"That's a nice nest," said the duck.
"Yes, it is," replied Chicken, "and I wouldn't swap it for *any*thing!"

More Andersen Press paperback picture books!

Ladybird, Ladybird
by Ruth Brown

What Would We Do Without Missus Mac?
by Gus Clarke

The Perfect Pet
by Peta Coplans

Peter's Place
by Sally Grindley and Michael Foreman

Dilly Dally And The Nine Secrets
by Elizabeth MacDonald and Ken Brown

Two Can Toucan
by David McKee

Happy Rag
by Tony Ross

Bear's Eggs
by Dieter and Ingrid Schubert

The Birthday Presents
by Paul Stewart and Chris Riddell

Frog And A Very Special Day
by Max Velthuijs

Dr Xargle's Book Of Earthlets
by Jeanne Willis and Tony Ross

Do Little Mermaids Wet Their Beds?
by Jeanne Willis and Penelope Jossen